Could Hannah be to blame?

Nancy raced back upstairs, brushed her teeth, and ran downstairs to the storage room to get the model of the pueblo.

Nancy was stunned by what she saw. The model was destroyed.

"Oh, no!" George cried. "I don't believe it!"

"It's gone! Our model of the Taos pueblo is gone!" Nancy cried. "Twigs and a few crumbs. That's all that's left."

Just then, Nancy noticed a worn, blue terry cloth slipper under the table. She couldn't believe it. It belonged to Hannah. Nancy was sure it hadn't been there yesterday. This was terrible. Would Hannah really have destroyed their project?

Join the CLUE CREW
& solve these other cases!

NANCY DREW
AND THE CLUE CREW®

#26

Camp Creepy

BY CAROLYN KEENE

ILLUSTRATED BY MACKY PAMINTUAN

Aladdin
New York London Toronto Sydney

This book is a work of fiction. Any references to historical events, real people, or real locales are used fictitiously. Other names, characters, places, and incidents are the product of the author's imagination, and any resemblance to actual events or locales or persons, living or dead, is entirely coincidental.

🪔 ALADDIN

An imprint of Simon & Schuster Children's Publishing Division

1230 Avenue of the Americas, New York, NY 10020

First Aladdin paperback edition May 2010

Text copyright © 2010 by Simon & Schuster, Inc.

Illustrations copyright © 2010 by Macky Pamintuan

All rights reserved, including the right of reproduction in whole or in part in any form.

ALADDIN is a trademark of Simon & Schuster, Inc., and related logo is a registered trademark of Simon & Schuster, Inc.

NANCY DREW and related logos are registered trademarks of Simon & Schuster, Inc.

NANCY DREW AND THE CLUE CREW is a registered trademark of Simon & Schuster, Inc.

For information about special discounts for bulk purchases, please contact Simon & Schuster Special Sales at 1-866-506-1949 or business@simonandschuster.com.

The Simon & Schuster Speakers Bureau can bring authors to your live event. For more information or to book an event contact the Simon & Schuster Speakers Bureau at 1-866-248-3049 or visit our website at www.simonspeakers.com.

Designed by Lisa Vega

The text of this book was set in ITC Stone Informal.

Manufactured in the United States of America 0310 OFF

10 9 8 7 6 5 4 3 2 1

Library of Congress Control Number 2009927732

ISBN 978-1-4169-9438-1

ISBN 978-1-4424-0605-6 (eBook)

CONTENTS

Camp Creepy

CHAPTER ONE

Project Pueblo

"And the team with the winning Native American model gets to spend the weeklong break at a camp in northern New Mexico!" Mrs. Ramirez announced. "In keeping with the spirit of the Native Americans, whatever you use must come from items around your house. This is a green competition."

"Wow!" Eight-year-old Nancy Drew whispered excitedly to Bess Marvin, who was sitting behind her. "That is so cool!"

"We have to build it first," Bess whispered back.

George Fayne leaned over from her desk

across the aisle from Nancy. "It's in the bag," she said. "I know exactly what we're going to do."

Their third-grade teacher, Mrs. Ramirez, had just told them that the uncle of their classmate Katherine Madison had bought a large summer camp near Taos, New Mexico. He had offered to let the winning team spend a week there over break—free of charge.

After the announcement Mrs. Ramirez called for quiet study time, but Nancy found it impossible to concentrate. She wanted to know what George and Bess thought.

George and Bess were cousins, though they didn't look or act anything alike. They were Nancy's best friends, and the three of them made up the Clue Crew. The Clue Crew was well-known at River Heights Elementary for solving mysteries.

Finally, the recess bell rang. With Nancy in the lead, the girls ran to a far corner of the playground.

"Now nobody can hear us," Nancy said. "What's your plan, George?"

"If we want to win this competition, we'll obviously have to focus on just one group of Native Americans," George said with a grin. "The Taos Indians. I saw a documentary about them last night on TV. I know all about their culture!"

"Taos!" Nancy exclaimed. "That's where the summer camp is."

"Exactly." George nodded.

"What if someone else chooses them?" Bess asked.

"We'll tell Mrs. Ramirez before anyone else does," Nancy said.

When the bell rang to end recess, Nancy and her friends raced back to their classroom.

"Excellent choice, girls!" Mrs. Ramirez said when they told her. "I'll put that down for you."

After school, as they headed back to Nancy's house, George said, "I printed a picture of the Taos pueblo from the Internet. I think it'll be easy to make." George was a whiz with computers.

Up in Nancy's room, George pulled out the picture. The building was three stories high and looked like wooden blocks stacked on top of each other. Each block was smaller than the one below it. "What's it made of?" she asked.

"Adobe," George said. "That's earth mixed with water and straw."

"I see wood sticking out at the top," Bess pointed out.

"Those are called cross-timbers," George said. "They help support the roof."

"Got it," Nancy said. "I know exactly what we can use."

Just as Bess opened her mouth to ask what, they heard barking in Nancy's backyard. Nancy walked over to the window. "Chocolate Chip has company," she said. "That's strange."

"What's strange?" George asked, joining Nancy at the window.

"I've never seen that other dog around before,"

Nancy said. "Hmmm. I wonder how it got in."
She turned away from the window. "Oh, well,
they seem okay. Let them play together. We
have work to do. We can see if the dog is still
there later."

As they headed downstairs, Nancy said, "We
have boxes and boxes of old wheat flakes cereal.
If we mix that with milk, we'll have the adobe,
and we can cut some dead twigs off one of the
trees in the backyard for the cross-timbers."

Right before they got to the kitchen, Nancy said, "I'll just tell Hannah we need the cereal for a school project, but I don't want to tell her *exactly* what it is."

"Don't you trust Hannah?" Bess asked.

"Of course, I do," Nancy said. "It's just that I don't want her to spill the beans! This is a competition."

Hannah Gruen was the Drews' housekeeper and had been with the family ever since Mrs. Drew died when Nancy was young. As a busy attorney, Nancy's father, Carson Drew, spent long hours both in his office and at the courthouse, which meant that Hannah's role in their family was more than just that of a housekeeper.

When the girls got to the kitchen, Hannah was looking out the window. "Where'd that dog come from?" Nancy asked.

Hannah wheeled around, startled. "What dog?" she said quickly.

"That cute little dog Chocolate Chip was playing with a few minutes ago," Bess said.

"I don't know what you're talking about," Hannah said. "Anyway, I can't talk now. I need to prepare dinner."

Nancy looked at Bess and George and raised an eyebrow. Why was Hannah acting so strangely? "Hannah, may I have some of those boxes of cereal that nobody eats?" she asked. "They're for a school project."

"Sure, sure, take whatever you want," Hannah said. "I never like to throw it away. I sometimes use it in meatloaf."

Nancy took three boxes of cereal from the back of the pantry. Then she opened the refrigerator and removed a carton of milk. "Take these to that little storeroom at the back of the garage," she whispered to George and Bess. "I'm going outside to get some twigs."

As Bess and George headed to the storeroom, Nancy started for the kitchen door that led to the backyard.

"Where are you going?" Hannah suddenly demanded.

"The backyard," Nancy said. "I also need some twigs for the project."

"Well, I can get them for you," Hannah said.

"We have to do everything ourselves, Hannah, or it won't be *our* project," Nancy replied. Something was definitely up.

Hannah relented with a sigh.

Outside Nancy looked around, trying to decide where to get the cross-timbers. Suddenly, she knew. One of the shrubs by the back fence had some dead branches. They'd be perfect. She hurried over to it. As she leaned down to break off the twigs, she noticed a hole under the back fence. It was too small for Chip to wiggle under and out of the yard, but it was large enough for the other dog to get in. She'd have to tell Hannah about it. But after she collected the twigs and went back into the house, Hannah was no longer in the kitchen. So Nancy forgot all about it and turned her mind to the project.

By the time Nancy got to the storeroom, Bess and George had already found a plastic bowl and had poured the wheat flakes into it.

"I think we should do this someplace else, Nancy," Bess said. "This place smells like an animal has been living in it."

Nancy sniffed. "No way, Bess. You're just imagining it."

Nancy poured some milk on the cereal in the bowl. "Now we get to squish it together," she said.

Once the mixture was the right consistency, the girls cut out the side of a cereal box to use as a base. They built the pueblo following directions George had found online.

George looked at the picture of the Taos pueblo, then at their model. "Perfect!" she said.

"Great idea, George!" Bess said. "I'm glad you saw that television show last night."

"Oh wait," Nancy said. "We need to use some of the twigs to build a couple of ladders. That's how they reached the upper stories."

They found some cotton string and tied different size twigs together to make the ladders.

"We'll leave it in here to let it dry overnight,"

Nancy said. She admired the model. "There's no way we're going to lose this competition."

George pulled a camera out of her backpack

and took a few pictures before she and Bess left. At dinner that night Hannah seemed more relaxed, and Nancy was so busy listening to Mr. Drew talk about his newest case, she forgot all about everything else.

It was only as she was about to get into bed that she looked out the window and saw Hannah running around the backyard in her robe that Nancy remembered the little dog. *Is this a home-grown mystery?* she wondered.

ChaPTER TWo

Picture Perfect

When Nancy woke up the next morning, she dressed quickly and ran downstairs to the dining room where Hannah had her cereal and toast ready.

"Thanks, Hannah!" Nancy shouted into the kitchen.

"You're welcome!" Hannah replied.

Nancy was just about to ask Hannah why she was running around the backyard last night, when she glanced up at the big clock on the wall and saw she was going to be late if she didn't hurry.

Nancy raced back upstairs, brushed her teeth, and ran downstairs to the storage room to get the model of the pueblo. The girls had agreed to meet outside Nancy's house and walk to school with the model.

Mr. Drew had left the garage door open. Just as Nancy reached the door to the storeroom, Bess and George arrived.

When Nancy opened the door, Bess said, "There's that smell again!" But Nancy was too stunned by what she saw to worry about any smell. The model was destroyed.

"Oh no!" George cried. "I don't believe it!"

"It's gone! Our model of the Taos pueblo is gone!" Nancy cried. "Twigs and a few crumbs. That's all that's left."

Just then Nancy noticed a worn, blue terry cloth slipper under the table. She couldn't believe it. It belonged to Hannah. Nancy was sure it hadn't been there yesterday. This was terrible. Would Hannah really have destroyed their project?

"How did this happen?" Bess cried.

"I know," George said firmly.

Nancy and Bess turned to her. Nancy wondered if George had seen Hannah's slipper too.

"What?" Nancy asked.

"I watched the second episode about the Taos Indians on television last night," George said. "This time it told about their beliefs."

"What does that have to do with the disappearance of our class project?" Bess demanded.

"The Taos Indians don't want other people to know anything about their customs," George said. "We angered one of their spirits when we built the pueblo, and that spirit destroyed it."

"Could something like that really happen?"

Nancy asked. She desperately wanted to believe that Hannah wouldn't destroy the model, though she couldn't think of any other reason why Hannah would be in the storeroom.

"Well, *someone* destroyed it," George said. "From what I learned last night, it's a definite possibility."

"What are we going to do?" Bess cried. "We don't have time to make another model before school starts."

Nancy was worried too. "I'm sorry," she said. "I'll take all the blame." There was no way she was going to ask Hannah about this, at least not yet. She just couldn't believe Hannah would do something like this. Still, she had been acting kind of strange yesterday. "It happened at my house," Nancy added. "So I'll be the one to tell Mrs. Ramirez that it was my fault."

"No," Bess said. "We're the Clue Crew. We stick together!"

"Bess is right, Nancy," George said.

Nancy sighed again. "Well, let's go to school

and get this over with," she said. "Maybe . . . Wait! I just thought of something!"

"What?" Bess asked.

Nancy looked at George. "The picture you took of the model last night," she said. "Maybe we could enter that in the competition! Do you have your camera with you?"

"Yeah, I was going to take pictures of the other models, too," George said. She opened her back-pack, took out her camera, and clicked until the screen showed their model of the Taos pueblo. "Oh, it would have won first place, hands down, and we'd be the ones going to New Mexico."

"We'll show Mrs. Ramirez the picture," Nancy said, "and maybe she'll let us enter the project from that."

"It's worth a try," Bess said. "Come on!"

When they got to their classroom, Nancy, Bess, and George hurried up to Mrs. Ramirez.

"Excuse me, Mrs. Ramirez," Nancy said. "We have a problem. We hope you can help us out with it."

"Well, I'll certainly try," Mrs. Ramirez replied. "What's wrong?"

"Well, we built a model of the Taos pueblo," Nancy said, "but it was destroyed sometime during the night."

Mrs. Ramirez raised a questioning eyebrow. "Really?" she said.

"Honestly," George assured her. "We have proof that we did the project." She took out her camera and showed the picture of the pueblo to Mrs. Ramirez. "We think it would have won first place."

"Even though we're all disappointed that we won't be going to the camp," Bess added, "we'd settle for a grade on the project."

Mrs. Ramirez looked at the picture closely. "Well, I can see by the time and date that this was taken last night," she said. "So I'll accept it for your project, but do you have any idea how this happened?"

"We think we made the Taos Indians angry," George explained. "Well, maybe not the people

16

themselves, but one of their sacred spirits."

"Well, I've never heard that excuse before,"
Mrs. Ramirez said. "That's really too bad. This
model certainly would have had a good chance
at winning."

"I just thought of something," George said.
"Do you think we could enter the picture in the

competition for the camp trip? After all, it's not our fault that it was destroyed."

Mrs. Ramirez grinned. "Well, I don't see why not."

Nancy and Bess looked at George. "Oh wow!" they said. "That's great!"

Nancy was surprised that her teacher agreed to let them enter the photo. First, Hannah was acting mysteriously and now so was Mrs. Ramirez. Could the two things be related?

CHAPTER THREE

And the Winner Is . . .

There was a knock on the classroom door. "Oh Mr. Madison! Please come in! We've been looking forward to your visit." Mrs. Ramirez waved the man standing in the doorway into the room.

"Uncle Doug!" Katherine Madison shouted. She jumped up out of her seat. "It's so good to see you! Where's Aunt Lucy?"

"She's back in New Mexico," Mr. Madison said. "She wanted to come, but we needed her back at the camp."

"Katherine, why don't you introduce your uncle to the rest of the class?" Mrs. Ramirez said.

"Everyone, this is my uncle, Douglas Madison,"

Katherine said. She was beaming. "I think he looks like a movie star."

At that, Mr. Madison blushed, but he also flashed a big smile.

"He really does," Bess whispered to Nancy and George.

"He could be in the Olympics too," George added. "That's very important for someone who's running a summer camp, because you have to be in charge of a lot of different sports."

"Let's be seated, class," Mrs. Ramirez said. She turned to Mr. Madison. "We're so glad you're here. Why don't you join me at the front of the room, and we'll get started. I know how busy you are."

"Well, I'm delighted to judge the projects,"

Mr. Madison said, "but I do need to fly back to Taos as soon as possible."

Nancy looked at Bess and George. "I wonder when she's going to tell him about the picture of our model?" she whispered.

"I don't know," Bess whispered back. She suddenly looked concerned. "What if he doesn't let us enter it?"

"Don't think negative thoughts, Bess! We have to win!" George whispered.

"As you know, we have a summer camp in the mountains of northern New Mexico, near the town of Taos," Mr. Madison said. "We're hoping to make it one of the premier camps in the country. I brought along a slide show for you, so you could see it all for yourself."

For the next several minutes, Mr. Madison showed the class slides of a big lake, which was used for swimming and boating, tennis courts, basketball courts, trails for hiking, and mountains for climbing. "We'll also have plenty to do indoors." He continued with slides of the craft room, theater rooms with stages where camp-ers can put on plays, the dining room, and the snack bar. As he came to the last slide, he added, "As you can tell, our camp has almost everything you can think of to make summer camp a special place." Mr. Madison paused and then, as Mrs. Ramirez turned on the lights, asked, "Well, how does it sound so far?"

"Great! Super! Fantastic! The best camp ever!" came the replies.

"Tell them the part about taking our pictures, Uncle Doug!" Katherine said, beaming.

"Well, the camp won't officially open till next year," he said. "The winners of the model com-petition will sort of be guinea pigs for us. We want to see what you like and what you don't."

"The pictures, Uncle Doug, the pictures!" Katherine said.

Nancy looked at Bess and George. "What is she talking about?" she asked.

"So while you're having fun, we'll have a pro-fessional photographer following you around,"

Mr. Madison continued, "taking photos that we'll use in a brochure we'll send all over the world."

"Oh that is so cool!" Deirdre Shannon said. "I'm planning to be a model, and this could be my big chance."

"You have to win first," Nadine Nardo said. "You have a lot of competition."

"Right!" Peter Patino said.

Mrs. Ramirez turned to Mr. Madison. "I think we need to start the competition."

Deirdre leaned across the aisle and whispered to Nancy, "Katherine will probably win. After all, it's her uncle."

"I don't think Mr. Madison would do that," Nancy whispered back. "He seems too nice."

Deirdre arched an eyebrow. "We'll see," she said.

"When I call out the names of the different groups, you may each bring out your model," Mrs. Ramirez said. "I'll help you place it on my desk for Mr. Madison to judge. Then the next group will go. Okay?"

Everyone nodded.

Mrs. Ramirez began calling names. Group by group, the class members presented their models. There were models of Mesa Verde in southwestern Colorado, the Chaco Canyon in northwestern New Mexico, a corn crop of the native peoples of the Eastern Woodlands, and even the Spiro Mounds in eastern Oklahoma.

Nancy looked at Bess and George. "I think we're in trouble," she whispered. "They're all really good." Suddenly, Nancy sensed that someone was looking at them. When she turned, she realized it was the entire class.

"Where's your model?" Deirdre asked.

For a few seconds no one said anything, then George held up her camera. "It's in here!"

There was some murmuring among the rest of the class.

"Class, Nancy, Bess, and George made a wonderful model of the Taos pueblo, but there was an accident," Mrs. Ramirez said. "Fortunately,

George took a picture, and I've agreed to let them enter that."

Several groans and even a few low-key protests were heard, but Mrs. Ramirez quickly said, "Put yourself in Nancy, Bess, and George's shoes, class. Wouldn't you want the rest of us to be understanding?"

The class agreed that that was the right thing to do.

For several minutes, Mr. Madison looked at the picture George had taken. Finally, he looked up at the class.

"Who's the winner?" Mrs. Ramirez asked.

CHAPTER FOUR

Repeat Performance

"You're *all* winners!" Mr. Madison announced.

There was a collective gasp from the class. Then everyone cheered.

Mr. Madison gave the class another one of his bright smiles. "Actually, I planned this all along with Mrs. Ramirez," he said. "I thought it would make you try your hardest to build the best model you could!"

"It worked, Uncle Doug!" Katherine said.

Nancy turned to Bess and George. "So that's why Mrs. Ramirez didn't seem too upset that we had only a picture of the Taos pueblo that we built."

"This is going to be super," George said.

Bess agreed. "It'll be just like a weeklong recess!"

As Nancy headed home that afternoon, she kept telling herself that if Hannah destroyed the model of the Taos pueblo, it must have been an accident. Maybe the reason Hannah hadn't said anything to her was she didn't know what it was. Maybe she thought it was just something that had been stored in the room for months— along with a lot of other junk they didn't want but didn't throw away.

At home Nancy headed straight for the kitchen for her after-school snack. Between bites Nancy told Hannah all about the week her class was going to spend at Mr. Madison's camp. She decided not to mention the competition.

From where Nancy was sitting at the kitchen table, she could see into their backyard. "There's that little dog again," she said to Hannah. "He's not wearing a tag. Where did he come from?"

"I don't know, Nancy," Hannah said hurriedly. "How about another cookie?"

Nancy looked puzzled. "You're going to let me have another cookie before dinner?" she said. Hannah never did that.

"Well, uh, I thought that if you, uh . . . ," Hannah stammered.

"What's wrong, Hannah?" Nancy asked.

"Nothing, nothing." Hannah said. She gave a

nervous giggle. "There's nothing wrong. Do you want another cookie?"

Nancy shook her head. "I think I'll go outside and play with Chip for a few minutes," Nancy said.

"No!" Hannah said. "I mean, why don't you go lay out the clothes you're going to take to camp, and I'll help you pack?"

Nancy hesitated. "Okay. That's a good idea. It'll help me decide if I need to buy some new things or not."

As Nancy headed upstairs to her room, she couldn't help but wonder what in the world was going on in her house. The model of the Taos pueblo had been destroyed, and Hannah was still acting strangely.

Three days later Nancy's class met at the River Heights Airport for the flight to Albuquerque.

"I wonder how far Taos is from Albuquerque?" George asked Nancy after the flight attendant had given them juice and a snack.

Nancy shrugged.

Mrs. Ramirez leaned across the aisle. "One hundred and twenty six miles," she said. "But Albuquerque is the closest major airport. We're taking a bus to Taos."

The bus ride was spectacular, taking the class through Santa Fe, along a steep gorge with the Rio Grande river at the bottom, and, just before they reached the camp, past a real Taos pueblo.

"Oh it's beautiful!" Nancy exclaimed. "The picture just doesn't do it justice."

"You're right," George said.

"I can't believe that it's been standing for almost a thousand years," Bess said. "That's amazing."

As they drove slowly past, Nancy noticed a boy about their age step from the shadows of one of the doorways. He had an angry look on his face, and he seemed to be staring right at her bus window. It gave her the creeps. *He knows about the pueblo we made in River Heights,* Nancy thought. *I'm sure he's telling me now that*

his people are very unhappy with us for doing that.

The bus finally arrived at the entrance to the camp, and the class was greeted by even more beautiful scenery.

"Those slides Mr. Madison had didn't show half of it," Nancy said. "Wow! A whole week here! I can't wait to get started."

The bus pulled up in front of the main lodge,

and Mrs. Ramirez and the class climbed off. The driver and some of the camp counselors pulled out the luggage from the storage underneath the bus. After picking up their suitcases and backpacks, everyone headed inside.

"Find your line for check-in," one of counselors shouted to them.

"We're in the *A* through *M* line," Bess said.

"I hope they let the three of us stay together," Nancy said.

As it turned out, Nancy, Bess, and George were grouped with Deirdre, Katherine, and Nadine.

"There are six of us to a cabin," Nancy said.

"Plus your counselor!"

Everyone turned. A girl with blond braids was smiling at them. "Hi! I'm Sincere!"

"Is that *really* your name?" Bess asked.

"Unfortunately," Sincere said.

"Are you?" George asked.

"Always," Sincere said with a grin. "What choice do I have? Right?"

They all gathered in the dining room for sandwiches and fruit, then Sincere showed the six of them to their cabin. Nancy was glad to see that it was larger than she had expected. There was plenty of room for the seven of them to have their own space.

After they unpacked, Sincere said, "Come on! Let me show you around camp. That'll help you decide what you want to do first."

The girls quickly put on their shorts, sneakers, and camp T-shirts and followed Sincere out of their cabin. The first place they headed was the lake.

"You can sail, or go canoeing, or swim," Sincere said. "Or you can simply lie out on the pier and enjoy the sunshine and the mountain air, but you'll need to make sure you put on plenty of sunscreen."

Just then Mr. Madison and a man with a big camera came up behind them. "Are you girls ready to have your pictures taken?" Mr. Madison asked.

"Yes!" Deirdre said. "Where do you want me?"

Mr. Madison smiled. "Well, I think we want *all* of you just to sit on the pier here and dangle your feet in the water."

"Are you sure the lighting is right?" Deirdre asked. "I photograph better in some lights than I do in others." She turned to the rest of the girls. "That's very important."

"Well, John here is a master photographer," Mr. Madison assured them. "He'll make sure

you all look really great—but since you already do, there's honestly not a lot he can do."

For the next hour Mr. Madison and the photographer followed the girls around the camp and photographed them in the woods, at the tennis courts, and in front of their cabin.

Finally, Sincere said, "We need to go to the lodge for a meeting about the Artisans Project."

"What's that?" Nadine asked.

"We're having each of the campers do a traditional craft. Camp artists will help you."

"Why are we doing that?" Katherine asked.

"Well, one of the things Mr. Madison wants is for the camp to have a market like the ones in Taos and Santa Fe where the Native Americans sell their art work," Sincere explained. "He thought it would be a great way to experience part of the culture of the area."

"I know just what I'm going to make," Nancy whispered to Bess and George.

"What?" they whispered back.

"Another model of the Taos pueblo," Nancy told them.

Bess's eyes went wide. "Are you sure it's safe to do that?" she asked. "You know what happened last time!"

ChAPTER FiVE

Watcher in the Woods

"We're a few miles from the real Pueblo, Nancy," George said. "It won't take an angry spirit long to get to this camp to destroy it, and then, well, who knows what else it might do?"

"That's just a chance I'll have to take," Nancy told them. "I have to know if all this talk about angry spirits is real."

Nancy and the rest of the girls followed Sincere to the main lodge.

"This is where the craft room is located," Sincere told them as they started up the wide wooden stairs. "We have everything you could possibly need to make your projects. The only thing you'll have to supply is your talent."

"When will the market be?" Nadine asked. "I hope it's not too soon, because sometimes my talent just isn't in the mood to make anything."

"In a couple of days," Sincere said. "So you might try giving it a little pep talk."

"What if the supplies I need aren't in the craft room?" Nancy asked. "What if I have to go somewhere else to get them?"

"Well, we'll see," Sincere said. "There should be *something* you can use around camp." When they reached the top of the stairs, Sincere said, "This way, girls!"

Just then, Nancy saw a young boy about their age coming toward them.

"Oh no!" Nancy whispered. It was the same boy who had stared at her when their bus passed the Taos pueblo before they reached the camp. "I don't believe it."

Bess and George looked at her.

"What's wrong?" Bess asked.

Nancy tried to say something, but he was getting closer and she didn't want him to hear.

As the boy approached their group, Sincere said, "Hey, Turkano! How's it going?"

"Hey to you, Sincere!" Turkano said. But as he talked to her, he never once took his eyes off Nancy. Was it possible that he knew what she was going to do?

After he left, Nancy caught up to Sincere and asked, "Who is that boy?"

"That's Turkano, Estefana's son," Sincere said.

"Estefana is the head chef for the camp. They live in the Taos pueblo."

A chill went down Nancy's spine. She was positive that the boy was somehow connected to the destruction of the pueblo model they made in River Heights. Was that look he gave her a warning not to do it again? And what did he want with Hannah?

Nancy hated keeping clues from Bess and George, but she wasn't ready to talk to them yet— what if Hannah really was involved in this in some way? She didn't want to get her in trouble.

When they reached the craft room, the rest of the class was already there.

"Look around," Sincere said. "See if there's something that interests you."

They each needed to make their own project. George chose to make a traditional basket, while Bess was making jewelry. Nancy was going to make another model, just like she said.

Nancy went up to Sincere. "I already know what I want to do, Sincere, but I'll need to go to a grocery store to get the things I need," she told her.

"Oh? There's nothing here you can use?" Sincere said. "What are you planning to make?"

"It's a secret," Nancy said. She hesitated. "Is it okay that it's a secret?"

"Of course it is," Sincere said. "I have to run into town. Do you want to come with me? We can stop by a grocery store before we leave."

"Oh that's great!" Nancy said. She hesitated. "I need to ask you a question, but I don't want to give away what my project is. Okay?"

"Okay," Sincere said.

"How much do you know about Taos Indian culture?" Nancy asked.

"I think I know quite a lot," Sincere said. "Not everything, certainly, but I read about it when I knew I was going to be one of the counselors here."

"Do you think it's possible for a person to make something that might anger one of their spirits?" Nancy asked.

"Well, if you're making something that is meant to be a gift to the native spirits, then I think you're fine," Sincere said. "But if you're making something that is meant to insult the culture, then I think you'll have problems."

"Oh I would never insult another culture," Nancy assured her.

"Then I don't think you have anything to worry about," Sincere said.

It took them about twenty minutes to drive into Taos. Sincere mailed a few letters, then she drove to a small grocery store they had passed along the way.

"I'll look at the magazines while you shop, Nancy," Sincere said. "That way your project will stay a secret!"

"Thanks, Sincere," Nancy said.

Nancy found the cereal aisle and bought three boxes of wheat flakes. She had already decided that instead of using twigs she was going to use pretzel sticks for the cross-timbers. That way, she wouldn't have to look around the campground and have people ask her what she was doing.

On the trip back to the camp, Nancy asked Sincere if she could drop her off in front of their cabin. "I'm going to work on my project there," she said. "It'll be a big surprise for everyone." Sincere agreed.

Just as Sincere dropped her off, Nancy spotted Turkano standing behind a tree down the road.

ChaPTER Six

Safely Hidden

As soon as Nancy got inside the cabin, she went to a front window and peeked out. But she didn't see Turkano out there anymore.

"I'm not doing anything to insult your culture," Nancy whispered. "You have to believe me!" Suddenly, she felt silly for talking to herself and letting a regular boy spook her!

Nancy turned back to her model. She really did think that she, Bess, and George had done a good job with the first model. She was sure she could duplicate that success and impress everyone at the market—and prove to herself once and for all that what she was doing was actually honoring the culture of the Taos Indians.

Nancy grabbed a plastic bowl from one of the shelves, took the milk from the fridge, honey from a cabinet, and put it on a table with the rest of the materials. She mixed the milk and the cereal to just the right consistency. Then she cut the sides of one of the empty cereal boxes, folded it inside out, and taped it together, so she could use it as the base for the model, just like they had done at home.

As Nancy started to form the sides of the pueblo, she heard a noise outside the front door. She froze.

The door began to open slowly. Who was there?

A head peeked cautiously around the door. "Are you okay?" It was Bess. George was behind her.

"Of course, I'm okay," Nancy said. "But you two scared me to death!"

"Sorry. We didn't mean to. We just came to check on you," Bess replied. "Do you need any help with the model?"

"No, but I think that boy—Turkano, you know, the one who passed us when we were going to the craft room—is spying on me."

George's eyes went wide. "Are you sure?" she asked. "Why?"

"Sit down," Nancy said. "I have something to tell you." Nancy told George and Bess about seeing the boy as they passed the pueblo when they were coming to the camp. "He knows about our first model of the Taos pueblo, guys. I think he's somehow involved in what happened to it."

"Really?" Bess exclaimed. "Why?"

Nancy nodded. "I think he thinks we're insulting his culture somehow."

"What are you going to do?" George asked.

"I'm going to make a perfect model of the pueblo," Nancy said. "I'm going to show him and his people that we meant no harm, that we were simply trying to show its beauty."

"Well, I'm almost finished with the jewelry I'm making," Bess told her. "I can stay and help, if you want."

"Same here," chimed in George.

Nancy shook her head. "I'll be all right," she said.

"Okay then, we're heading back to the main lodge," said Bess.

"Be careful!" George called.

The girls left the cabin and Nancy turned back to her model. She pushed the pretzel sticks through the upper walls, so she could make the roof. Then she poured some honey into another bowl, thinned it with some water, and spread it on the walls.

That should make them stay together better, she thought. She stood back and admired her work. Suddenly, she had an idea. *I'll let the model dry for a while. Then I'll ask Sincere to help me find Turkano and get to the bottom of this.*

Nancy looked around the cabin. Where could she leave the model to dry, undisturbed? She opened several closets until she thought she found the perfect one. It was in a far corner of the cabin and had pillows on the top shelf. Nancy grabbed a chair to stand on. Moving aside a couple of pillows, she set the model as far back as she could on the shelf and then carefully hid it with a pillow.

When she finished, she shut the closet door and put the chair back by the desk.

Nancy quickly put away all of her supplies, then looked around the cabin to see if she had left any telltale signs of what she had done. When she was satisfied, she headed out to rejoin the rest of the crafters.

Suddenly, she heard a loud crash on the roof!

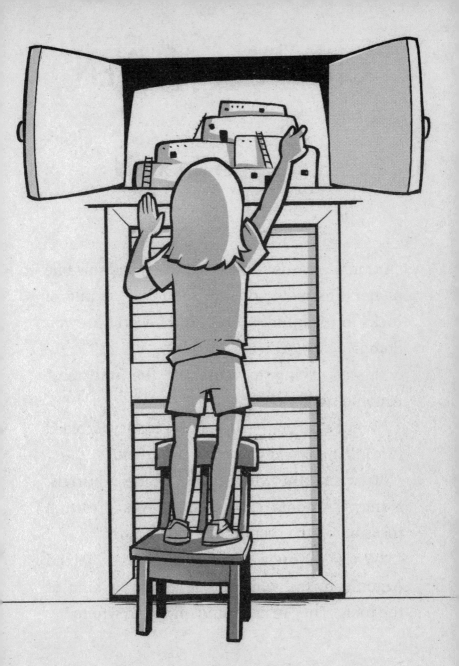

CHAPTER SEVEN

Enough Is Enough!

"Antonio Elefano!" she cried when she saw one of her classmates on the road with a pile of rocks in his hand. "What in the world are you doing?"

"I was trying to scare off the squirrels," Antonio said.

"What's wrong with you?" Nancy scolded him. "Why would you try to hurt them?"

"I wasn't throwing rocks *at* the squirrels, Nancy," Antonio explained. "I was throwing rocks up on the roof to scare them away."

"Why?" Nancy asked. She had joined Antonio in the yard and was now looking at the roof. "They're not doing anything wrong."

"Maybe not now, but they might if they come down the chimney and start tearing up your cabin, looking for food," Antonio explained. "That's what they did to ours. You should see the mess."

"Oh as long as you're just scaring them away, then I guess that's all right," Nancy said.

Just then, Nancy saw Bess, George, Deirdre, Katherine, and Nadine heading toward them.

"Hey, I was just heading back to the lodge," Nancy called. "What's up?"

"We've finished our projects," Katherine replied. "We're all going swimming in the lake. We came to change."

"That sounds like fun," Nancy said. "Antonio, go tell the boys in your cabin to put on their swim trunks and join us."

Within minutes the girls had on their bathing suits, with their beach towels wrapped around them, and were headed for the lake.

"I'm cold," Deirdre said.

"It's this mountain air," Katherine said. "It's

not as warm here this time of year as it is in River Heights."

"We'll warm up once we're in the water," George told them.

Sincere and the other counselors were waiting for the campers down at the lake. They waved to Nancy and the other girls.

"How's the water?" Bess called.

"It's great!" Sincere shouted. "If you're a polar bear!"

As it turned out, the water wasn't that cold, and Nancy, Bess, and George relay raced Antonio, Peter Patino, and Quincy Taylor. With George swimming the final lap, they won two out of the three contests.

Finally, Bess said, "My teeth are chattering! I need to get out!"

"Not me," George said. "I'm just getting warmed up."

"I'll come with you, Bess." Nancy joined Bess on the pier.

"This is fun, isn't it?" Bess said, as they

sunned on the pier. "Maybe we could come next year for real."

"You never can tell," Nancy said. "I think . . ." She stopped. "Look, Bess," she whispered. "There he is."

"There *who* is?" Bess whispered back.

"Turkano, the one whose mother is the head chef," Nancy said. "He's hiding over there in the trees. I'm sure he's *stalking* us."

Bess's eyes widened. "What are we going to do?"

Nancy thought for a minute. "I have an idea. If I could just talk to him, then I think maybe he'd understand, and then maybe he could explain it to whomever . . ." She stopped. "Where did he go? He just disappeared." Before they could look for him, they were interrupted by George. "Hey! Everyone's coming back to the pier," she shouted to them, pointing to her waterproof watch. "It's almost time for dinner."

"We need to hurry if we want to shower first," Nancy said. "I want to wash off this lake water before we get dressed for dinner."

Together, Nancy, Bess, and George hurried up the hill toward their cabin.

Once they got back, Bess and George started to get ready, but Nancy wanted to show them her model first. "After you see it, I think you'll agree no one will be destroying it this time," she said.

Nancy went to the closet where she had hidden the model. She climbed up on a chair and took down the pillow she had put in front to hide it.

"Oh, no! Oh, no!" Nancy cried. "I don't believe it."

Bess and George rushed over to her. The model looked like it had been attacked.

"Somebody is really angry with you, Nancy," George said.

"And Nancy knows who it is," Bess told her. "That boy, Turkano!"

"*What?*" George cried.

Nancy pulled the cardboard base from the shelf and showed them. "Well, it's not all gone, just some of the walls," she said. "It's not like what happened in River Heights."

Just then they heard the rest of the girls coming up to the cabin. Nancy quickly put the model back on the shelf and put the pillow in front of it. "Maybe I can repair it before the market," she said.

"Nancy!" Bess cried. "Enough is enough!"

"She's right, Nancy," George said. "If you don't stop, then maybe next time, well . . . I don't even want to think about what might happen to you."

CHAPTER EIGHT

Sincere's Snack

Nancy was the last one to get dressed. Bess and George waited for her while the other girls went on ahead. The Clue Crew had a lot to talk about.

"I'm sure Turkano is responsible for this," Nancy said. They left the cabin and headed for the dining room at the lodge. "I should have walked right up to him and explained what I was doing."

"It might be better to drop the whole thing," George said.

"George is right, Nancy," Bess added. "You should just think of something else to make and sell at the market."

At the moment the market was the last thing

on Nancy's mind. She needed to find out what really happened to her model, but right now they needed to rush or they'd be late for dinner.

They joined the other kids in the camp's dining room. Surprisingly, the food at the camp was super good, and everyone was murmuring their approval.

"Well, I'm glad you like it!"

Everyone turned to see who said that. A woman in a white coat and a tall chef's hat had come up to their table. "Hello," she said, "I'm Estefana Lake Talk. I'm the head chef here at the camp, so I'm always delighted to hear nice comments about the food."

That must be Turkano's mother! Nancy thought. She wanted to say something to her about the pueblo and ask her why her son wanted to destroy it. Before she could, though, Mrs. Lake Talk turned to her and said, "You're Nancy Drew, aren't you?"

Nancy gulped. How did Mrs. Lake Talk know that? "Y-yes," she managed to say.

"I have a son, Turkano, who has some things he wants to say to you," Mrs. Lake Talk said. She looked around. "He was here a few minutes ago, but I don't see him now." She smiled. "He appears and disappears all the time."

"What did he want to talk to me about?" Nancy asked. George and Bess were staring eagerly as well. "Can you tell me?"

"I don't think I should," Mrs. Lake Talk replied. "I'll leave it to him to explain." She turned to the rest of the girls. "Well, enjoy! We're so glad you're here!"

With that, she turned and headed for another table.

"That was super mysterious!" Bess said.

"Yeah," Nancy agreed. "The next time I see Turkano, we're going to settle this once and for all."

"Be careful, Nancy," George cautioned.

Back at the cabin Sincere had some card games she wanted to teach the girls, but Nancy was too distracted to play. She put on her pajamas and got into her bed. From where she was lying, she could see outside one of the windows into the woods. The moon lit up the landscape.

As she lay there, she thought about the market and Turkano's possible involvement in destroying her model. She would have to try to fix it to prove to him she wasn't doing anything wrong. Plus she didn't want to let Mr. Madison down.

The next morning Sincere and the other girls left the cabin for breakfast, just as Nancy, Bess, and George began getting dressed.

"Come on, lazybones!" Sincere called on her way out. "We'll see you in the dining room."

Nancy wanted to consult with the Clue Crew while the others were out of the cabin. "Maybe I should just go ahead and try to repair the model?" she said.

"Nancy! You're tempting fate!" George said. "What if it just happens again?"

"Well, I have another plan," Nancy told them. "I'm not going to let this model out of my sight. If Turkano tries to destroy it, he'll have to take it from me, and I'll do everything to make sure that doesn't happen."

George shook her head. "I don't know about this," she said. "How will you carry it everywhere?"

"Yeah, Nancy," Bess agreed.

"I've made up my mind," Nancy said determinedly. She pulled a chair over to the closet where the model was, climbed on it, and took away the pillow.

"Bess! George!" Nancy cried. "It can't be!"

Bess and George rushed to her. Nancy lifted the cardboard bottom, took out the model, and held it where they could see it. "More of the walls are missing!" Nancy said. "In River Heights the *whole* model was gone the next morning, but now it keeps disappearing a little at a time."

"Put it back, Nancy!" George said. "Put it back right now!"

"Why?" Nancy asked.

"Don't you see?" Bess said. "They're telling you something!"

"*Who's* telling me something?" Nancy said. "I want to know!"

"We have to leave the cabin now," George said. "I don't think it's safe for us to be here!"

"George's right, Nancy!" Bess said. "This is no ordinary crime." Bess looked pale. "We've never tried to solve a crime where the criminals are . . . are . . . are . . . *invisible*. They could be anywhere!"

"You think it's the spirits?" Nancy looked nervous.

George nodded solemnly.

Nancy, Bess, and George hurried out of the cabin and ran to the dining hall. They ate breakfast in a corner, by themselves, since most of the class had already finished.

Mrs. Ramirez came up to them and said, "Are you girls all right? I haven't seen you around much."

"We've been busy with our art projects for the market," Nancy told her. "We want to make sure they're the best."

"Let me know if I can help," Mrs. Ramirez said. She looked around. "Isn't this a wonderful camp? I am so happy that Mr. Madison invited us."

"We are too," the Clue Crew chorused.

After breakfast Nancy, Bess, and George wandered around the camp in awkward silence.

They just didn't feel comfortable going back to their cabin.

Finally, Nancy said, "This is silly! We're the Clue Crew!"

"We solve mysteries!" George said. "We're not afraid!"

"You're right!" Bess said. "We can solve any mystery!"

"I'll go ahead and repair the model," Nancy told them. "It probably won't sell, but I'll have entered something at least." George and Bess nodded.

After Nancy picked up some art supplies at the craft room, they headed back to their cabin.

When Nancy opened the door of their cabin, though, the first thing she saw was Sincere. She was propped up on her bed with several pillows—munching on something that looked suspiciously like the walls of the Taos pueblo model!

CHAPTER NINE

Turkano's Secret

"Sincere!" Nancy gasped. "Why are you eating that?"

Sincere gave the girls a puzzled look. "Are you kidding me? If you had ever tasted Lucy's granola bars, you wouldn't be asking that question!"

"*Granola bars!*" Nancy, Bess, and George gasped in unison.

Sincere sat up. "Yeah! Lucy is one of the camp counselors here." She grinned. "She probably thought I wouldn't find them, but I did, and these are her best ever! Besides the cereal, there are pretzel sticks and a hint of honey."

"Where exactly were they?" Nancy asked. She swallowed hard.

"You'd never believe me," Sincere said. "They were on a shelf behind the extra pillows." She grinned again. "Lucy probably thought they were safe, but I needed a couple of extra pillows. When I got them, I found the granola bars." She got a puzzled look on her face. "What I don't understand, though, is why she made them in the shape of a box!"

"That was my model of the Taos pueblo," Nancy told her. "It's what I planned to sell at our market."

Sincere gasped and almost choked on a piece of the pueblo wall.

"Oh no, I am so sorry!" she said. She threw the remaining pieces on the ground. "I had no idea."

"Is this the first time you've eaten it?" George asked.

"No, I ate some yesterday," Sincere said sheepishly. "Why?"

Bess turned to Nancy. "Well, this mystery is solved," she said, "but that still leaves the mystery of what exactly happened to the first model."

Sincere gave them a puzzled look. "What do you mean?" she asked.

Nancy, Bess, and George told Sincere about the model they had made in River Heights.

"It was all gone, though, not like this one, where you just ate the walls a bit at a time," Nancy said. She thought for a second. "You didn't have anything to do with the disappearance of that one, did you?"

"No, I've never been to River Heights," Sincere said. "That *is* kind of strange though."

"We thought they were both destroyed

because we had angered some of the Taos Indian spirits," George said.

Sincere looked at Nancy. "So that's why you were asking me all those questions!"

Nancy nodded.

"Well, I guess we could ask Estefana about it." Sincere stood up. "She's probably still in the dining room."

"I don't know if that's a good idea," Nancy said. "Her son has been spying on me since we arrived, and Estefana even told me that Turkano wanted to talk to me about something important."

"Nancy's not making that up, Sincere," George said. "Turkano has been watching us, like he was just waiting for the right moment to do something."

"You thought he wanted to tell you *not* to build a model of the pueblo?" Sincere said.

Nancy nodded. "Or *destroy* it!"

"But maybe you ate the second one before he could," Bess suggested.

"I hadn't thought about that, Bess! Good

detective work," Nancy said. She turned to Sincere. "We really should go talk to Estefana and get to the bottom of this."

When they reached the lodge, Sincere led them back toward the kitchen. Just as they started to push open the swinging doors, Turkano burst through them.

Turkano blushed when he saw them, but Nancy marched right up to him.

"Your mother said you have something you

wanted to talk to me about," Nancy said. "Is that right?"

Turkano nodded. "But I don't want to bother you with it, if you're busy."

"Does it have anything to do with a model of the Taos pueblo we made in River Heights?" George asked.

Turkano looked puzzled. "Huh?"

"You didn't know about that?" Bess eyed him cautiously.

Turkano shook his head.

"Well, why were you spying on me, then?" Nancy asked. "I saw you hiding behind those trees."

"I wasn't spying on you. I was just trying to get up the nerve to ask you a question," Turkano said. "Mr. Madison told me about you, and I wanted to find out how I could be a detective too."

Nancy blushed. "That's it?" She looked at Bess and George.

"I've always wanted to be a detective," Turkano

said. "After Mr. Madison told me that you're one, I asked Katherine and she said you're the best."

"Maybe you can help us with this case. Do you know any reason why Taos Indian spirits might want to destroy a model of the Taos pueblo?" Nancy asked.

Turkano frowned. "What? No," he replied. "Why?"

Nancy shrugged. "I don't know," she said. She turned to Bess and George. "Well, we've solved the mystery of what happened to the second pueblo model, and now we've solved the mystery of why Turkano was watching us, but that still leaves the mystery of what happened to the first pueblo."

"Some mysteries just never get solved," Turkano told them.

"If that happens, it'll be the first case the Clue Crew hasn't solved," George said. "I don't like the thought of that."

The camp market was held the next day. Nancy raced to complete the model in time, but she couldn't. Meanwhile, both George's basket and Bess's jewelry sold well.

"Don't be upset," Bess said. "If Sincere hadn't eaten your model, it would have sold for more than both of ours together."

"Thanks, Bess," Nancy said, "but your jewelry and George's basket were great."

"I do think it's nice that Sincere gave the camp some money for the model she ate," Bess replied.

"Yeah," George said. "That was a really expensive granola bar!"

At a loss for how to explain the River Heights disaster, Nancy, George, and Bess did their best to enjoy the rest of their time at camp.

Finally, the day before they were scheduled to leave, Sincere called the girls over. "I wish you'd make another model of the Taos pueblo. All of the market items the people in Taos bought have been donated back to the camp to be displayed in showcases to inspire future campers."

"Turkano said it wasn't the spirits, and it wasn't him, so . . ." Bess started.

The girls looked at each other. "And we're so close, at least we can get all of the details exactly right," Nancy said. "Let's do it!"

That evening, after they finished their third model and put it out to dry, George said, "If something destroys this model during the night, we know for sure this case isn't closed."

ChaPTER TEN

Everything's Gone
to the Dogs!

A knock at the cabin door awakened Nancy early the next morning. She heard Sincere talking to someone. When Sincere came back inside, she was holding a piece of paper. "Nancy, a message arrived for you last night and they forgot to bring it over."

Sincere handed Nancy the paper.

"Bess! George!" Nancy cried. "Daddy spent last night in Santa Fe! He's driving up to the camp this morning!"

"Is there something wrong?" Bess asked sleepily.

Nancy smiled. "No, no. It's a surprise! We're driving back in an RV with him," she said. "But he's taking us to Canada before we return to River Heights!"

"Oh wow!" George said. "That is so cool!"

"I can't wait to show him the model when he gets here!" Nancy cried. She raced to the closet where she had put it last night. Quickly, she pulled up a chair to the closet and moved the pillows aside.

"It better still be there," Bess remarked.

"Whew," Nancy told them. "It's still here! I think the curse is finally broken."

"Thank goodness." Sincere winked.

Nancy pulled the model down and set it on the table.

"I'll stay here with you until you father arrives," Sincere said. "You can show him around when he gets here."

Just then they heard barking outside the cabin.

"That's odd," Sincere said as she opened the cabin door. "There are no dogs in camp."

"It can't be!" Nancy cried. Through the

doorway Nancy could see a little dog. And just beyond, parked in front of the cabin, was Mr. Drew's RV. "Daddy!" Nancy shouted.

Suddenly, before Nancy could move, the little dog raced up the walk, into the cabin, and leaped first onto Nancy's bed, then the table. Right away he began eating the model of the Taos pueblo!

"Stop! Stop!" Nancy cried. "That's supposed to be for . . ." She didn't finish. She turned to see Bess and George looking at her. Without saying another word, they started laughing so hard they couldn't catch their breaths.

"I think we just solved the River Height's mystery," George gasped.

"I knew that storeroom smelled like an animal had been in it," Bess said. "We should have followed my lead!"

"You're right, Bess," Nancy managed to say. "The clue was *licking* us in the face!"

Just then Mr. Drew appeared at the door. "Oh no, Nancy, girls," he said. "I'm so sorry."

"It's all right, Daddy," Nancy said, giving him a big hug. "We just solved the last part of the Taos pueblo mystery!"

Mr. Drew looked puzzled. "Well, that's good . . . I guess."

"Is that dog the same one that was in our backyard before we left for camp?" Nancy asked.

Mr. Drew nodded.

"Why is it with you, Daddy?" Nancy said.

Mr. Drew rolled his eyes. "That's a very long story," he said. "Maybe I could tell you over breakfast."

"I'll lead the way," Sincere said.

"What'll we do with the dog?" Bess asked.

"I'll have one of the other counselors show it around the camp," Sincere said.

"That'll work," Mr. Drew said. "It's been cooped up in the RV since River Heights, and it's ready for some exercise."

Once the dog was in good hands, they all found a table in the dining room.

"This food looks great," Mr. Drew said. "This is like a resort."

Between bites of pancakes, eggs, and bacon, Mr. Drew told everyone the story of the little dog. "When Hannah first saw him in the backyard, she couldn't believe it. He looked just like a little dog she'd had when she was a child that had run away. She knew she couldn't really keep him, but he didn't have a collar and didn't seem to belong to anyone, so she wanted to make sure she found him a good home. She was trying to keep the dog a secret until then."

"That explains why she was acting so strangely!" Nancy interrupted.

"Yes," continued Mr. Drew. "But right before I left for New Mexico, Hannah was called away to help a sick relative. Although Chocolate Chip likes to go to the kennel, Hannah thought the little dog might feel abandoned again and asked me to take him on the trip."

"What're you going to do with him now?" Bess asked.

"When we get back to River Heights," Mr. Drew said, "we'll have to find him a permanent home."

"Look no further!"

Everyone turned. Mr. Madison had been standing by the table, unnoticed. "We've been wanting to find just the right dog for the camp," he said, "and this one sounds perfect."

"Hannah will be thrilled!" Nancy said. "The dog will have a good home, and when we come back to camp, we'll get to visit him!"

"There's still one thing you have to do, Nancy," Sincere said.

Nancy looked puzzled. "What's that?" she asked.

"You promised you'd make a model of the Taos pueblo for the camp craft display case," Sincere said.

Everyone groaned.

Finally, Nancy said, "All right, but just as soon as I finish it, we're going to lock it inside the case."

"Agreed!" Sincere laughed.

"Another mystery solved," said Nancy. "Let's get started on the fourth—and last—model!"

Make Your Own Adobe House

Adobe is a natural building material made from clay, water, and sand mixed with straw. People have been using adobe for thousands of years to build houses. Many Native Americans in the American Southwest live in adobe houses, much like the model Nancy, Bess, and George made. Now you can make one too!

You will need:

Newspaper

A big plastic mixing bowl

A piece of sturdy cardboard (from a box)

A small paintbrush

Wheat flakes cereal

Enough milk to moisten the cereal, so you
   can mold it

Pretzel sticks

Honey diluted with water

❁ Lay out the newspaper to cover your work surface; this will make clean up easier later.

❁ Pour one box of cereal into the mixing bowl and add enough milk to make your "adobe clay." It should be the consistency of mud.

❁ Next, using the "adobe clay," form four walls for the adobe house. The walls should be about five inches long, about a half inch thick, and about two inches high. Let the walls dry for a couple of minutes.

❁ Carefully push the pretzel sticks from one wall across to another wall, just below the top. Make sure the ends of the pretzel sticks show from the outside of the house, so they will look like cross-timbers. You'll need to use several pretzel sticks and keep them close together so they will support the roof.

❁ Gently put some of the "adobe clay" on the roof.

❁ Let the adobe house dry for a couple more minutes, then use a pretzel stick to punch out a small door and a couple of small windows.

❀ Finally, use the paintbrush to brush the house with the diluted honey to help hold it together.

Now you have an adobe house like those in which many Southwestern Native Americans live—and perhaps a tasty treat for your pet as well!

If you want to create a model pueblo, follow the steps above several times, making each adobe house smaller so you can stack them one on top of another.

Nancy Drew and The Clue Crew

Test your detective skills with more Clue Crew cases!

FROM ALADDIN • PUBLISHED BY SIMON & SCHUSTER

NANCY DREW
AND THE CLUE CREW®

Can you solve these other mysteries from Nancy Drew and the Clue Crew?

Collect them all!